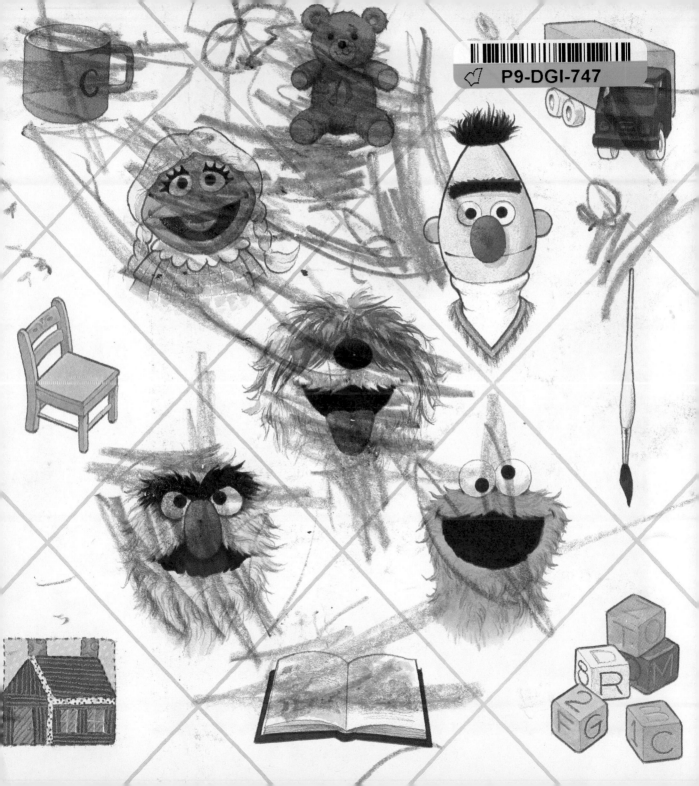

A1

B2

C3

4C

Scared of the Dark

By Liza Alexander/Illustrated by Tom Cooke

Featuring JIM HENSON'S
SESAME STREET MUPPETS

A SESAME STREET / GOLDEN PRESS BOOK

Published by Western Publishing Company, Inc. in conjunction with Children's Television Workshop.

F G H I J

One Saturday Ernie and Bert went to the movies. They caught the matinee at the Bijou. The feature was *Ghosties*.

It was twilight when Ernie and Bert started walking home.

"Ernie, wasn't it scary when the Ghosties invaded the bedroom and grabbed the boy and flew him out into the night?" said Bert. "Yikes!"

"Yeah," said Ernie, but he wasn't really listening. He thought he saw something crouching behind a streetlamp, but it was just a garbage can. Ernie shivered and began to walk faster.

ONE WAY

"Or what about the part, Ern," said Bert, "when the boy opened the refrigerator and instead of his bologna sandwich, he found…snarling Ghosties? Cool, eh? Heh, heh."

"Yeah, sure, Bert," said Ernie, peering into the basketball court as they passed it. The shadows looked dark and deep. "Anything could be hiding in those shadows," thought Ernie.

Later that night, after supper–even with a cup of cocoa with marshmallows–Ernie didn't feel like going to sleep.

"I think I'll stay up a little longer, Bert," said Ernie. "Maybe I'll work on my model airplane, or look at a book, or watch TV, or something…"

"Ernie, don't be ridiculous," said Bert. "It's bedtime. Now get into your pajamas and brush your teeth and go to bed."

Soon Bert was snoring, but Ernie couldn't sleep. His eyes were wide open. In the dark he watched the headlights of a passing car flash silver across the wall.

Then Ernie saw something behind the door. His body tensed. His eyes grew wider.

Ernie's mind raced. "It's a monster," he thought, "with a huge head, and long tangly hair, and one long gigantic arm, and he's going to grab me. Oh, no!"

Ernie gulped, but very quietly so that the monster wouldn't hear. Ernie tried not to breathe or even blink his eyes so that he wouldn't make the monster mad.

Ernie couldn't take it any more. "Bert!" he screamed.

"Ernie," said Bert, "whatever is the matter?"

"Don't go over there!" yelled Ernie. "There's a monster behind that door."

Bert turned on the light. "Look," he said. "There's no monster over here. It's just a coatrack with all your junk hanging on it."

"Okay, Bert. I guess you're right. But it did look like a monster," said Ernie.

"Fiddlesticks!" said Bert. "No wonder you're scared of the dark. You forgot to take Rubber Duckie to bed with you. Now just settle down, Ernie. Count sheep or something. Let's get some shut-eye."

Ernie hugged Rubber Duckie tight and tried counting sheep, but he still couldn't sleep. Then Ernie heard a low hiss. He didn't rustle the blankets or move or make any kind of noise at all.

"Boy," thought Ernie, "Bert is lucky that I'm still awake and have such sharp hearing. Something fishy is going on here."

Ernie noticed that the closet door was open a crack. "I knew it," thought Ernie. "Something bad is in there and it's going to ooze out and..."

"...YIIII!" screamed Ernie. He bounced right onto Bert's bed.

"B-B-Bert, there's something in the closet and it's going to slime out all over us."

"Oh, Ernie," said Bert. "There's nothing in the closet. See?"

Bert walked up to the closet and opened the door. There was nothing in there but shoes, clothes, and junk.

"But what about that hiss?" said Ernie. "Listen."

"Yes, Ernie," said Bert. "I hear it. That hiss is the radiator."

"I guess you're right, old buddy," said Ernie.

Bert rummaged around in the closet. "This might help," said Bert. "A night light! Then the room won't be so dark."

The soft glow of the night light made Ernie feel cozier. But then he thought he felt something move under the bed. Ernie stretched himself out. "Now whatever is under here won't see any bulges and won't attack," he thought.

"There could be a big snake with fangs slithering under there," thought Ernie, "or maybe a shark swimming around looking for something to eat. Aaaaargh."

"What am I thinking? There's nothing scary under this bed. A shark would need water, and snakes don't live on Sesame Street."

Ernie took a deep breath, leaned over, and looked under the bed. "Okay," Ernie said to himself. "Now just take it easy and try to get some sleep."

The harder Ernie tried to go to sleep, the harder it was to get to sleep. Ernie listened to the wind outside whooshing through the trees. He watched shadows dancing across the wall. The shadows reminded him of something.

"They're coming," thought Ernie. "They're waiting in the trees. They're going to fly in the window...and grab Bert...and fly him into the night! And then they'll snatch me! Here come the..."

"GHOSTIES!" screamed Ernie.
Ernie's scream was so loud
that it knocked Bert right out
of bed.
"Oh, Ernie!" groaned Bert.

"Bert! You woke up just in time," said Ernie. "The Ghosties are invading Sesame Street."

"Er-nieeeee! All I see on that wall is shadows," said Bert. "The tree outside our window is tossing in the wind. See? It throws the light from the streetlamp all crazy against the wall, and makes wild shadows.

"Look, if I close the curtain all the way – no more Ghosties."

"Ernie," said Bert, "your imagination is acting up tonight. It must be that scary movie we saw."

"I guess so, old buddy," said Ernie.

"Why don't you imagine nice things instead of scary things," said Bert.

"Like what, Bert?" asked Ernie.

"Imagine it's summer and we're at the beach," said
Bert. "You're floating over gentle waves on your
inflatable seahorse. Just relax, Ernie."

Ernie forgot about the Ghosties. Imagining nice things, he drifted off into a sweet sleep.

The next morning Ernie whistled as he fixed his favorite breakfast, Monsterberry Crunch with milk and bananas. Bert dragged into the kitchen.

"Hey there, old pal," said Ernie. "How are you feeling this wonderful morning?"

"I am very tired, Ernie. I didn't sleep a wink. Thank you very much."